CHAPTER 36

Two weeks later, the Twelveworld Lord and the Courser Lord announced their arrival by walking into the cargo bay. Surela was in the middle of a meal with the Chatcaava; the sight of them caused everyone to rise, but it was for her to extend an invitation as the head of the wing. "Twelveworld Lord. Escutcheon-Prime. Please, join us."

Without fanfare, the two sat to the table, and conversation resumed; as this revolved around the training programs Lead-Systems had reinstated to keep everyone occupied, the talk was innocuous. When the meal concluded, no one expressed surprise when Lord Haladir said, "Viper, we would have words with you."

"Yes, sir," she said—in Chatcaavan, as he had addressed her, and because he addressed her as he would a wing lead. She followed him and the Twelveworld Lord out of the bay, and from there to the empty mess. Ra'aila had known about their arrival, because she'd left a coffee service prepared, and pointedly used the Laisrathera porcelain.

In keeping with his personality, the Twelveworld Lord availed himself of the dainties and stimulants; the Chatcaava were not dessert-eaters by nature, but the Twelveworld Lord had adopted the habit with enthusiasm when among aliens, and brought back a plate scattered with berries and something that looked like a custard. Seeing it, Lord Haladir murmured in Eldren, "Pony."

"I'm not round as one yet," the Twelveworld Lord replied cheerily. He reversed one of the chairs and straddled it to allow his wings room, reminding her powerfully of the first time she'd met him in this very room. "So, Viper. We come bearing news of a compromise, arrived at by all three nations. We hope it will meet with your approval!"

Haladir set his face in one hand and was gently rubbing his brow. "Huntbrother...."

"What? She's made it clear she will fight to defend her wing. I honor her for it." The dragon smirked at her, switching to Eldren so he could shower the words with various extreme mood modifiers, all black or stormy-shadows. "The Lord of War was wroth. And now my huntbrother will say I am coming it a little too strong, and yet! I am not!"

Haladir leaked a laugh. She thought. He smoothed his hand down his face and said, "Hear now the command of your Empress, Surela Silin. The dragons in your charge have been sentenced and found guilty of sedition against the Chatcaavan Empire, and their superior officers of crimes against humanity by the Alliance. As soldiers answering to those officers, the members of your wing are guilty of complicity with those orders... however the complication of their personal oaths and their material aid to you and Alliance citizens in escaping the creatures known as epigones, has resulted in the commutation of their sentences. They are to be exiled to the Eldritch Empire, there to be disposed of as the Empress sees fit. We have suggested they become members of the community at Imthereli, which already has a Chatcaavan population."

"What do you think?" the Twelveworld Lord asked. "Will it serve?"

"You ask me?" she said, startled.

"You have placed yourself between everyone and those Chatcaava," Lord Haladir said. "And you have taken that charge seriously. Of course we ask you."

"Then... I will say that I will put it to the wing," she said, slowly. "They may not want to be exiled. If they choose instead to be executed... would that be permitted?"

"It would be," the Twelveworld Lord said. "And I'll kill them myself if they want to take the coward's way. Oh, don't look at me that way, Viper. It is the coward's way. Your people and ours are similar enough for an Eldritch to fight his way to the third pillow, bed the Emperor *and* his Queen, and plant his dragon children on Eldritch soil under his banner. There is a rich and challenging life awaiting any male who accepts 'exile' here. If they can't see it, then I'll open their miserable throats without qualms."

Haladir cleared his throat. "I would not quite go so far... but I will say that having delivered this verdict, the Alliance isn't interested in the fate of your wing. They wanted Apex-Fleet, not a handful of underlings. Putting a sensor technician on a galactic stage for punishment lacks the drama the Pelted craved as justice for the loss of Tam-ley. They would prefer to make much of the body of Apex-Fleet and the wreckage of his fleet than to chance that someone will feel pity for some ship's mechanic."

"It was very quietly decided," the Twelveworld Lord agreed, sipping his coffee with exaggerated care to keep from spilling it from the Pelted-designed cup. "I suspect there were several private conversations along the lines of 'this wasn't what we wanted, can we make this disappear.'"

"Providing it does disappear," Haladir said. "The quicker we escort these Chatcaava to their new habitation and give them identities as Eldritch citizens, the better." He folded his hands together on the table and said, "When I say soon, I mean now, Mistress. If you must confer with your wing, please do that. The Twelveworld Lord and I will enjoy the *Earthrise's* hospitality while we wait."

She stood. "I go immediately, my lords."

———

WHEN SHE STEPPED through the cargo bay doors this time, all the Chatcaava rose to face her. She did not call for the council because all of them were owed the knowledge. "You have been reprieved," she said. "They do not require your execution. Rather you are to be exiled to my people's care, to live in their kingdom." She hesitated, then said, "It is a small one, for now, with only two solar systems in its keeping, but it is growing. And you will find company of your own kind, for the settlement to which they suggest you go is Imthereli, which is composed of a great number of Chatcaava."

"Is that your settlement?" said one of the males.

"No," Surela said. "I am a tenant of another House, Laisrathera, which owns and operates this merchant vessel."

Thenok nodded, the Eldritch gesture. "I would prefer to answer to you, Viper. Would that make me part of Laisrathera? Is that a choice we can make?"

"I... I don't know," Surela admitted. "I feel constrained to reveal that I am exiled from Eldritch soil for crimes I committed against its empress. I serve Laisrathera abroad because I cannot set foot on the planet or any of its stations."

"This vessel is not considered Eldritch soil though it is owned by an Eldritch house?"

"My liegelady is human," Surela said. "It's... complicated."

"Then," Staff-Prime said, "Please, sit, and explain it."

"Yes," said Thenok. "Because we are navy, Viper. What use would we be on a planet?"

"We could build things, maybe?" said another.

"Could we become citizens or do we remain prisoners?"

"Stay you," Surela said. "And I will summon the Twelveworld and Courser Lords. These are questions I cannot answer alone."

If the latter males were surprised to be pulled into this impromptu meeting they hid it well. But the questions taxed even Haladir's Eldritch reserve, which, Surela was forced to acknowledge, had never been more than modestly adequate. He must have fared poorly at court, though when she strove she couldn't remember much about him, save that he'd been more often in male company than in the palace flirting with females.

"All these things can be negotiated," Staff-Prime said at last, "except for the most important. The Viper took our part when we needed defense; she accepted us as her wing at the behest of our last commander, and executed that role to our satisfaction. We wish to remain part of whatever she's part of. If I understand this correctly, we are limited in that interaction by the terms of her sentence... and ours, because if she cannot go to the Eldritch worlds, and we cannot go into Alliance space, then we can't meet. The best we can do is to pledge to her commander. Do I understand correctly?"

"Yes," Haladir said. "Assuming that is well with her liegelady. That would make you part of Laisrathera."

"That is where the child lives," said one of the males. "And she makes mention of Chatcaava."

"There are some Chatcaava in Laisrathera," Haladir agreed, and arched a brow. "The child?"

"Mine," Surela said. "She's made friends of them all."

"She is charming," Thenok said. "She reminds me of my youngest sister."

"You should go call your lady," the Twelveworld Lord said heartily. "And yes, right now." He beamed at the Chatcaava. "I don't want to leave your people exposed, Viper. Go take care of it."

"Yes, sir," Surela said, resigned to his amusement, and beginning to find the situation funny herself. She could now; as she strode to her cabin, she allowed herself to realize what she was feeling was respair: that she hadn't been exiled again, and the dragons who'd saved her life, and Saul's and Fassy's, and all the Alliance prisoners'... they weren't going to die. What had those quiet conferences been like? Between the Emperor of the Chatcaava, her Empress, and whomever the Alliance had put in charge of the diplomatic correspondence?

Theresa answered immediately. "Surela! You have no idea how happy I am to see you today."

"I can imagine, somewhat," Surela said, "since I am as glad. And for any discomfort I might have caused you, and am about to cause you, I apologize."

"Oh, it was fine—wait, about to cause me?"

"My Chatcaava would prefer to become tenants of Laisrathera rather than belong to Imthereli. They feel some loyalty to me and I have explained that pledging to you is the closest they can come to staying mine."

For several moments, Theresa gaped at her... and then she chuckled. "Oh, gods, Surela. Really? Should I be telling

Liolesa not to worry about you accruing a Chatcaavan army?"

"No," Surela said firmly. "I am entirely yours, and hers. I nourish no ambitions save to serve the Eldritch's aims."

"I know. Sediryl told her too, when she came back. You know she came to evaluate you."

"I imagined so."

Theresa nodded. "You made a favorable impression, which didn't surprise me. And it's worked out for the best, or at least, as much of the best as we could expect from the situation. The Alliance's more concerned with the slides—the wormholes—and their makers than they are with joggling the Emperor's elbow while he's fighting a civil war. Or at least, Fleet is, and it's surprising how much power Fleet has."

"Perhaps not, given that Fleet would be prosecuting the war against the Empire. Again."

"Probably. Anyway, Liolesa's pleased with how things fell out, which means she's pleased with me. And that means..."

Surela smiled. "You are pleased with me."

"Yes. So if you want me to adopt your dragons, I'll do it. And I'd be happy to give you another terrifying gift, if you want one. Do you? Don't say you want to keep Lunet because of course you can. Something else."

"My lady," Surela said, meaning it, "you have given me everything already." Seeing the mutinous light in Theresa's eyes, she finished, "But if I think of aught else, I will tell you."

"Good. Go tell your dragons to pack. I'll get Irine on quarters for them until they decide where they want to live. Unless they want to work in orbit... we wouldn't mind the help there. If they can be trusted?"

"They saved my life when they still thought me a wingless freak."

Theresa nodded. "Benefit of the doubt, then." She smiled crookedly. "I'm in for another bout of teasing about rescuing people who need second chances, I imagine."

"Deservedly, my lady," Surela said. "And we honor you for it."

It was only after the channel had closed that Surela dared to think that the word she'd really wanted was 'love.' They loved Theresa for it. She thought the Chatcaava would too.

In the cargo bay, she said, "It's settled. Laisrathera is pleased to welcome its newest immigrants. I cannot accompany you there, but...."

"We will," the Twelveworld Lord said. "We'll be glad to show you the sights. And the females." His eyes sparkled. "The prettiest Chatcaavan women are found in this system, my friends, and all of them are a challenge. You're not going to be sorry."

CHAPTER 37

"Well," Danica said, "it's good to be back. Doing the farewell tour was a little depressing, so I'm glad it wasn't necessary after all."

"The... what?" Surela asked.

Meri set plates out on the mess table, nodding. "I did it too. Wandered the station, looking at all the things I might not see again. I took a visit to Reese's place, even, and spent an afternoon by the ocean. I really like your oceans, Rel, they're nothing like what I expect. All those slow, high waves. It makes you feel like you're in a dream. And you get the craziest fogs, sometimes. Everything on your world feels a little like a picture book. I'd miss it if I couldn't see it again."

"I like the trees," Prudence said shyly. "Even trees I think I recognize are taller than I expect. Like the Eldritch are to humans, your trees are to normal trees."

"But... I'm sorry. You make it sound as if you might not have ever seen them again."

"Of course we did," Erynne said. "If they'd decided to

punt you into a whole other empire, it would have been over."

"You're part of the crew," Danica said. "More than that, you're the Eldritch who's our symbol of why we're in this job. We're attached to watching this system grow. Most of us don't have that chance to see anything like it, you know? The Alliance is built up already. Unless you get yourself signed up for a colony, and there's no guarantee a colony initiative will open in your lifetime."

Meri nodded. "Your Eldritch explorer lady would tell you that, I'm sure. Part of the reason she's out there, that any of us do any mapping, is to find worlds suitable for colonies, and they're always special because—"

"They're rare," Erynne finished. "Dani's right. I signed up for this job because I wanted to indulge myself in a little small-ship tinkering before I got stuck managing some high end cruise ship's maintenance department. But I stayed because it's been breathtaking watching Cradle just... blossom. I didn't think it would happen so fast. You blink, and something new's happened."

Leo brought a cake out of stasis and set it on the counter alongside the carafes, and his silence was so unwonted that Surela asked, "And you? Also feel this way?"

The Harat-Shar wrinkled his nose. "It's always about the people, Rel."

When Surela looked at Ra'aila, the Aera shrugged. "What did you expect? That we'd stay on for a paycheck? A lot of us might have showed up initially because we weren't sure what to do next with our lives. But we stayed because you people really are as charming as you're glowed up to be."

"You're the symbol of that, the daily reminder of why we do it," Danica finished.

"A mascot!" Meri said.

Muffled from beneath the counter, Leo objected. "I wanted to be the mascot!"

"Too bad," Erynne said, grinning. "Rel looks better on posters."

"All right, won't argue that."

"You would really have left if I'd been exiled?" Surela repeated, astonished and touched.

"Obviously," Danica said. "And if you didn't realize that...."

"But we get to keep you!" Leo exclaimed.

"And Lunet!" Meri added.

"Oooh, yes, and Lunet," Erynne said, rubbing her hands together. "I'm going to turn your daughter into an engineer yet, arii."

"I'll go get her," Meri said. "Hopefully Saul's finished parading her around the station. She wanted lemon ices for the party."

"Lemon ices, and cake?" Danica asked, ears askew. "Isn't the cake some kind of chocolate coconut thing?"

"More dessert is always better," Leo chirped.

As the *Earthrise's* crew finished preparing for a celebration Surela hadn't realized they'd been hoping for because the alternative had been either the dissolution of their fellowship, or its exile, Ra'aila wandered over and rested a hand on the back of Surela's chair. Quietly, the Aera said, "You're not surprised, I hope."

To be surprised would have been to reject the evidence of years of camaraderie. She could not pretend not to know the depth of their devotion to one another, and to her, without dishonoring them. So she said, "I am grateful, rather. That you have welcomed me to your company, and that you commit yourselves to my people. But I wouldn't have expected or required any sacrifice, Ra'aila."

"No," Ra'aila said. "And if you had, you wouldn't have gotten it out of us. Which is how it usually works."

"And how long will you stay?" Surela asked.

"I don't know. Hard to tell what the future holds. But I think as long as we feel like we're making a difference, and we're part of something bigger than we are…" Ra'aila smiled. "It's not so much my thing, because we like roaming, Aera, and my clan in particular. But we have it on good authority that your Empress welcomes Pelted immigrants, and Reese has been good to us. Some of us have been talking about that. What it would be like to settle down in Laisrathera, maybe start a family. There are big Tam-illee and Harat-Shar communities already on your planets, and Forecourt's got a pretty mixed population."

"Goddess," Surela said, startled. "Are you serious?"

"It's been ten years," Ra'aila said. "It's good work. And you're good people and the world's gorgeous. I bet your other planet's as interesting, and I'm sure it won't be the last one. Who wouldn't want to be part of a growing concern? Especially nowadays, when the Alliance is focusing on forting up? You don't get the same sense of wonder and excitement in the Core anymore, and the colonies are agitated about what might happen to them. This… this place is an oasis."

"That may change," Surela murmured.

"Maybe. But your people don't seem to be closing their eyes to threats, arii. They're just assuming that they can overcome them. The Alliance is still reeling from the realization that they can be hurt. Like someone who's never been in a fight getting punched for the first time."

Surela watched Meri set out glasses. "You'll return to the fight, wiser for the experience."

"I hope so. But it's hard not to prefer to be in the company of the scarred-up duelist who's already got the sword out and waving, saying 'was that all you've got.' And that's without adding the dragons. This is the only place I know of where the Chatcaava and the Pelted aren't barely tolerating one another." Ra'aila shook her head. "No… I think you underestimate how good you've got it here. But trust me, we aren't."

"That is not tea-wine," Surela said as Leo showed up at her side to pour.

"It is!" Leo said. "I got it from our employer. She said we should celebrate. It's Nuera, which is supposedly the best."

"There's even a watered glass for the baby girl and… here she is!" Danica scooped up Lunet as the girl darted through the hatch. "Hello, kara!"

"Eee, a party! My favorite thing! And with cake! I brought the ices, just like I said I would!" Lunet waved a bag over Danica's arm. "Look, Mother, ices! For our dragon friend!"

On the threshold, Thenok looked abashed beside Saul. "I greet you all," he said in careful Universal. And then in Chatcaavan, "Thank you for inviting me."

"You invited him?" Surela asked Ra'aila.

"Of course I did," Ra'aila said. "He's crew now."

"What…!"

"So long as I do not disembark at any Alliance facility," Thenok said, "it was determined that I am not breaking the terms of my exile. We discussed it amongst ourselves and decided we would rotate through month-long shifts, if it was well with your captain, Viper. So that you need not go unprotected by us. We asked our new commander and she said it was well by her, so long as we did not leave the ship."

Ra'aila, ignoring Surela's pointed look, sipped from her glass. "I said yes."

"So now we get to have Chatcaavan company!" Lunet exclaimed. "Isn't that wonderful, Mother? It's nice to have more than one of us aboard. And your wing is so nice! Thenok said he would play counting games with me so I can improve my math."

With the desserts set out, and the wine, and all the crew seated, Ra'aila said, "We've got about a week's liberty before they send us out again, probably back to Ro for farming equipment. Get all your errands wrapped up before then. Until and unless I hear something different, it's business as usual."

"Here's to business as usual," Danica said, raising her glass.

———

"It doesn't bother you?" Surela asked Ra'aila later at the door to her cabin. "To be hosting one of the Chatcaava responsible for Tam-ley."

The Aera sighed. "If I think of it that way, of course it does. And if they were enthusiastic about killing off wingless freaks, I'd dump them not only off the ship, but out an airlock. All's fair in war, and all that. But that's the thing, isn't it? It was war, to them, and us. And now the war's over and we have to live with one another. We have to figure out how to move on. Maybe this is my way of doing that... and maybe it's theirs, too." She shook her head. "All I can say is I'm glad I didn't have to make this decision about the traitor who gave the order. Him being dead already was the best thing that could have happened to us."

"Do you think so?"

"Oh yes. Ends the chapter definitively. Time to tap the page and see what's next."

She thought about that in her cabin while she waited. About the difficulty of making peace with the past when the past included error and malice. Theresa had told her once that Surela-the-Traitor was not so important an individual that her death was required to heal from the wounds of the coup, and the human had been correct. But Apex-Fleet had reached a different conclusion. Perhaps it was because the war could not be considered ended until his fate had been resolved? Or maybe it had been as simple—and as complex —as the Traitor still harboring some sense of loyalty to the male who would be placed in an impossible position by his survival. The male who'd recorded the final, vitriol-filled message had borne no relation to the leader who'd been concerned entirely for his remaining people, the male who'd been willing to embrace the Change to survive, the one who'd fought at her side to protect not just his people, but the Alliance prisoners he'd brought up the rear to oversee.

History would make a villain of him entire. Alliance history, anyway. Perhaps even Chatcaavan, if the Emperor decided it served them. Who would remember him as something other than the caricature? If not her? Who had also been a traitor?

The door chime raised her from her reverie, and she said, "Come," for Saul, who didn't enter all the way. He leaned on the door, arms folded, and since he was waiting for her to begin, she said, "So, you need not make any dire and irrevocable choices after all."

"Would it have been either?" He smiled a little. "I hear the Empire's an interesting place for foreigners these days. They've even got a bunch of Eldritch there, if the broadsheet's right."

And it had never entered her mind, that exile to the Empire would have delivered her to Imthereli's growing coterie on the throneworld. Would the head of House Imthereli have welcomed her as an asset to his court? Or would he have held her at swords' length, knowing her history and being, if gossip held any truth, far less tolerant of trespass?

"As for irrevocable," Saul said, "I don't know. Nothing's certain under the suns, except that we live and die. Lot of room for change between those two points. In fact, I'd say that's the only other certain thing. Change."

"You would have given up your homestead on Escutcheon?"

That gave him pause.

It was not a guess on her part. The moment Ra'aila had spoken of the crew's considering Eldritch citizenship, she'd known.

Gently, she said, "You could ask your cousin by. Perhaps she'd come."

"Maybe she would," Saul answered, voice rough. "Maybe she will." A smile then, creasing half his mouth. "What's Leo always saying? It's about the people. It's always about the people." Then he lifted a brow. "Don't assume I'd be the only one who'd have gone, either."

The idea that the *Earthrise* crew would decamp for the Chatcaavan Empire to follow her was so absurd she refused to linger on it. Her heart would break and stay broken, and Goddess knew what would grow out of the pieces. At very least she would find it impossible to face them over a breakfast table, knowing that she'd inspired such devotion. Had she remained an Eldritch noblewoman she would have known how to respond to such confessions of loyalty... what was she supposed to do as a dispossessed supercargo on a merchant vessel? And now she had—apparently!—added a coterie of some fifty dragons to their number! "What am I to do with you, Master Saul," she said at last, torn between exasperation and something far too rich to be called fondness.

"God willing, you'll have plenty of time to figure it out." He grinned and saluted. "Good night, Rela."

"Good night, arii."

Not long after, Lunet arrived, yawning and holding Bippity in her arms. "Oh, Mother," she said. "I do believe I've overdone the celebrating. And the sweets."

"A good time for sleeping, then. Go wash up, child."

For once, Lunet did not spend forever primping before exiting the head and climbing wearily into bed. Even her wings dragged at the blankets, rumpling them. Surela tucked Bippity under one of the girl's arms and pulled the covers over her. "There. Shall I sing you the lullaby about the girl and the sea?"

"Are you going to sleep?"

"Not yet," Surela said. "I have some correspondence to catch up with. And I'd like to think a while."

"Ohhh. I know how that is. Thinking is so much easier alone, isn't it?" The girl yawned, showing a gaping mouth and little sharp teeth. They were unfairly adorable; truly, motherhood shifted one's perspective in every conceivable way. "You don't need to sing, Mother. I know you're near and that's good enough. I like sleeping while someone else is awake...."

"I understand." Surela kissed the smooth brow. "Rest gently, sweet one."

She did stay up a little longer. Thinking of the crew. Of the Chatcaava. Of Apex-Fleet, and politics. Of the creatures that had longed to roam the universe and wreak desecration on it, and Fasianyl—and Goddess, she hadn't even found out if Fasianyl had been reunited with her musician. She smiled a little. She wasn't sure she believed in 'plenty of time.' But tomorrow was soon enough to call and ask. And tomorrow, she thought, she could count on.

APPENDICES

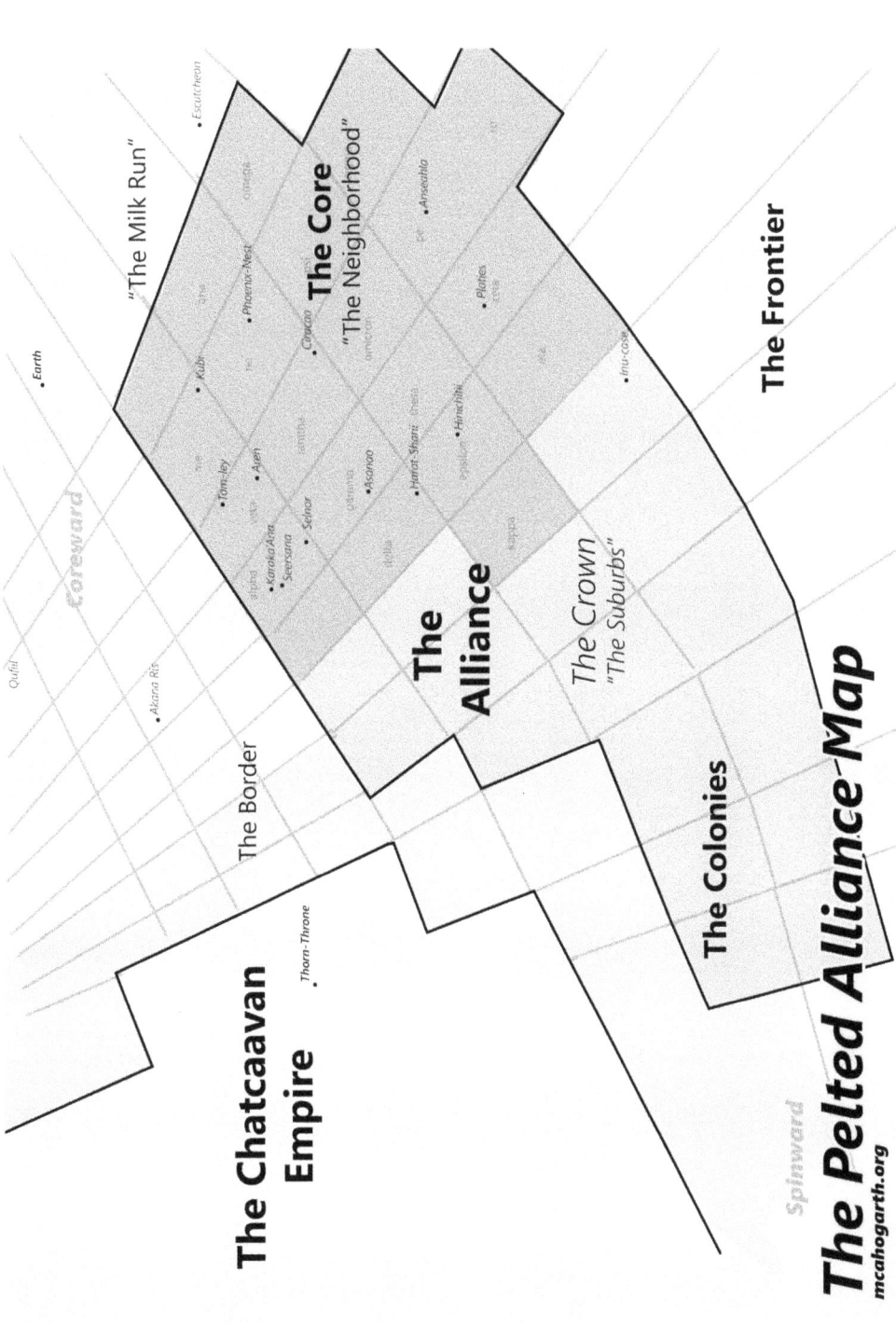

THE SPECIES OF THE ALLIANCE

Three major groups of sapients are known to exist in the Peltedverse (so far): **the Pelted**, who founded the Alliance, and who are the descendants of animal-human bioengineering experiments on earth; **humans and their offshoots**, the Eldritch; and the **true aliens**, who evolved naturally on alien planets. A fourth, minor group, **AI**, is filled solely by the sapient evolution of AI in the Alliance network.

The following, alphabetically, is a list of known peoples, with graphics.

- **Aera (Pelted)** – This brightly colored race is tall, hare-eared and long-muzzled like foxes, and tends toward nomadic cultures. Some variants also have winged ankles.
- **Akubi (Alien)** – The Akubi are giant bird-like/dinosaur-like creatures, nine to twelve feet tall, with thick razor beaks and large wings. They have three sexes, and the neuters are the ones that tend to travel to see the interesting little mammals. They are excellent mimics and enthusiastic observers of alien culture.
- **Asanii (Pelted)** – One of the more numerous of the core Pelted races, the Asanii are plantigrade people with humanoid faces, but a veneer of domestic feline. They have five fingers and toes, catlike tails, and nails rather than claws. They are excellent jacks-of-all trades, socially and skills-

wise, thanks to a culture that emphasizes mutability.
- **Birdsong Natives (Alien)** – Not much is known about the natives of planet Birdsong, who are not part of the Alliance.
- **Chatcaava (Alien)** – A species of shapeshifters, in their natural form, the Chatcaava look like bipedal winged dragons. Some females are also winged, but most have two sets of arms rather than arms and wings. They sat on the other side of a cold war with the Alliance for a long time, and their Empire is substantially larger than the Alliance thanks to an expansionist warrior culture permeating the upper echelons of their society.
- **Ciracaana (Pelted)** – A race of gengineered centauroids, the Ciracaana are very tall, very lanky, and have furred and pawed lower bodies with long tails and faces with pointed muzzles and large pointed ears. They come in any number of riotous colors and patterns. They were another of the three races created by the Pelted in an attempt to understand their origins.
- **Crystals (Aliens)** – Not much is known about the crystal people, who were found on a single moon and have made no move to join the Alliance or leave their habitat. Their first (and only significant) mention is in *Earthrise*, the first book of the Her Instruments trilogy.
- **D-Per (AI)** – Digital personalities started out as AI assistants in the early Alliance and evolved to more complex and sapient forms.

- **Eldritch (Human Family)** – The Eldritch are an offshoot of humanity, altered with greater longevity, light gravity bodies that are long and delicate, and uniform skin and hair color and texture (pearl and fine/straight, respectively). They are one of the only known esper races in the universe.
- **Faulfenza (Alien)** – This heavy-gravity world race is tall, furred, powerfully muscled, standing on digitigrade legs. They have muzzled faces and long ears that fan open, long tails with two tufts, and six fingers/toes. A race of dancers, they are also gifted with the Mindfire, which allows them to burn/heat things with their hands.
- **Flitzbe (Alien)** – The alien Flitzbe are plant-like creatures that reproduce via budding and photosynthesize for energy; they communicate

empathically and travel in clods that stick together using their flexible neural fur. In appearance, they look like small furry basketballs that change colors.
- **Glaseah (Pelted)** – The second of the two engineered centauroid races, the Glaseah are compact, dense people with the lower bodies of great cats and a humanoid upper body with a short-muzzled face and feathered ears. All are skunk-patterned; some have membranous wings on their lower body, and some don't. A phlegmatic and practical people, they were the last species created by the Pelted in an attempt to understand their origins.
- **Guardkin (Quasi-Pelted)** – The Guardkin are the result of centuries of breeding for intelligence by the Hinichi, who consider themselves the Guardkin's caretakers. They resemble wolves (or larger wild dogs) and can bond to espers to make their minds known.
- **Harat-Shar – (Pelted)** The party people of the Alliance, the Harat-Shar are big-cat-based, and can be either plantigrade with finger fingers and toes and nails, or digitigrade with four fingers and toes and claws. They can have any big cat pattern, though some are more common than others.
- **Hinichi (Pelted)** – Built primarily from lupine additions, the Hinichi are the wolf-like people of the Alliance, clannish and stubborn and noble. They can be plantigrade, with five fingers and toes and nails, or they can be digitigrade with four fingers and toes, and claws.

- **Human (Human Family)** – Our descendants. Humans from Earth come in the expected shapes, sizes and colors... there are also Martian humans (short but tending toward less mass) and Lunar humans (very ethereal thanks to their light gravity builds).

- **Karaka'A (Pelted)** – The Karaka'A are another felid race, domestic cat-biased, but they're all short, with digitigrade legs and four fingers and toes and claws. Because they were offshoots of the very first Pelted experiments (which were foxlike), they can have fox-like patterns as well as catlike ones.
- **Malarai (Pelted)** – A small populace, the Malarai were built off the Asanii base (humanoid with thin veneer of cat) with feathered wings grafted

on. Their feathered wings are too small to fly with in normal gravity, and their original design left them with a predilection toward lower body disorders, mostly nerve but sometimes joint-based.

- **Naysha (Pelted)** – The most alien of the gengineered races, the Naysha are mermaid-like creatures, with the lower bodies of porpoises and the upper bodies of humanoids, with heads that are somewhat otter or seal-like, with enormous eyes. Lacking the apparatus for speech, they speak via sign.
- **Octopi (Aliens)** – A relative newcomer to the Alliance, the octopi aliens look like enormous octopuses with translucent veils connecting their limbs. They are one of the two inhabitants of the planet Amity; the second, the sapients who lived on land, have died out. Their first contact story is told in the Stardancer novel *Either Side of the Strand*.
- **Phoenix (Pelted)** – The Phoenix are mammalian bipeds with birdlike features, like long beaks and crests and feathered wings and tails. They were engineered by the Pelted, who subsequently found them more alien than many of the true aliens. They come in any assortment of metallic colors.
- **Platies (Aliens)** – Another sea-based alien, the Platies look like colorful flatworms, except without mouths or eyes or any visible organs. They begin palm-sized and can grow to the size of a shuttle. They communicate only with the Naysha, who can't explain how that

communication works, and are capable of traveling by folding space (also poorly understood). Some Platies can be found on Fleet warships as adjuncts to the navigation/propulsion systems.

- **Seersa (Pelted)** – The other elder Pelted race, the Seersa are short fox-like people, digitigrade with four fingers and toes and claws. They can have fox or domestic cat patterns, being very similar, biologically, to their sister-race the Karaka'A.
- **Sirelanders (Alien)** – The Sirelanders are a nomadic race of aliens that never stops traveling the universe. They wandered through the Alliance and kept going, though there are Alliance anthropologists who are tagging along with them to study them.
- **Tam-illee (Pelted)** – The last foxish race of the Pelted are the Tam-illee, who are also the most humanoid of the group. They have five fingers and toes and nails, and stand plantigrade, and have human-like faces with fox ears and fox tails. The Tam-illee are also one of the few Pelted races that can often be born completely furless.

DRAMATIS PERSONAE

Being a brief catalog of major and minor characters in the novel. More information can be found on the peltedverse wiki at peltedverse.org.

Araelis Mina Jisiensire. Eldritch. The current head of House Jisiensire, which was nearly destroyed by Surela's liegeman Athanesin, Araelis defied Surela when she was briefly queen, and was one of the first to make her question her beliefs. Araelis appears first in the novel *Rose Point*.

Athanesin Fesa Sovanil. Eldritch. The liegeman who razed the province of Jisiensire, purportedly in Surela's name. His misdeeds and their effects on Surela's short reign are chronicled in the novel *Laisrathera*. He was executed for his actions by the Lord of War, Hirianthial.

Baniel Sarel Jisiensire. Eldritch. The former High

Priest of the Eldritch Church, Baniel consorted with pirates and slavers in order to bring down the Eldritch monarchy. He used Surela as a catspaw in his plans. His story is told in the Her Instruments series, and he appears first in the novel *Rose Point*.

Basilisk. Human. Pirate. Dangerous, but not more so than a dragon.

Breath of the Living Air/Chatcaavan Queen. Chatcaavan. The consort of the Chatcaavan Emperor is only briefly mentioned in this novel as the woman who pardoned the Twelveworld Lord for his treasonous acts. Her evolution from powerless slave to the most powerful woman in the Empire begins in the novel *Even the Wingless*.

Danica Blakesley. Karaka'An. First mate of the TMS Earthrise at the time of *Exile*. She herds cats, that's why Ra'aila hired her.

Emperor (Chatcaavan). Chatcaavan. The head of the Chatcaavan Empire had a redemption arc from villain to great moral power even more extreme than Surela's. His story begins in the novel *Even the Wingless*.

Erynne Seyvald. Asanii. Golden-haired engineer of the TMS Earthrise at the time of *Exile*. Competent and always ready to fix the things.

Haladir Delen Galare. Eldritch. The father of the current heir to the Eldritch Empire (Sediryl Galare), and currently the head of the nascent Eldritch Navy. Divorced from Sediryl's mother, Thesali Nuera Galare. He appears briefly in Sediryl's origin story novel, *Girl on Fire*, and again in his own novel, *Fathers' Honor*.

Hirianthial Sarel Eddings Laisrathera (once Jisiensire). Eldritch. The Lord of War, and Theresa Eddings's husband. He was instrumental in the defeat of Baniel, Surela, and the pirates, and in the restoration of Liolesa to her throne, and has significant history with her which is described in the novel *Rose Point*. *Rose Point* is also the novel where Hirianthial meets Saul Ferry.

Leo (Leonid). Harat-Shar, lion-based intrarace. Purser on the TMS *Earthrise* at the time of *Exile*. Heart of gold, complete with flaky-looking exterior.

Liolesa Galare. Eldritch. Queen and later Empress of the Eldritch Empire. The story of the coup she defeats with her various allies is told in the Her Instruments series, starting with the novel *Earthrise*.

Lunet. Chatcaavan. Daughter of Surela Silin Asaniefa. A winged shapeshifting dragon girl, remanded to House Laisrathera's, and Theresa Eddings's, care.

Maia. D-Per ("digital personality"). The sentient AI hired by Empress Liolesa to help her manage the Eldritch expansion. Maia made her in-canon debut in the Princes' Game series, in *Amulet Rampant*.

"Meri" Merina York. Pilot of the TMS *Earthrise* at the time of *Exile*. Inexhaustibly curious and always learning.

Mina Brown. Karaka'An. A Fleet intelligence agent, partnered with Montie Dawson. She and her partner are currently stationed in the Eldritch system to lend their aid to the Empress.

Montie Dawson. Human. A human intelligence asset on loan to Fleet, Montie and his partner Mina have made sporadic and mysterious appearances (as is proper for their profession) throughout the events of the war. We first meet them in the collection *Major Pieces*, however, in the short story "Jackal Chest."

Prudence MakesShift. Tam-illee. Healer on the TMS *Earthrise* at the time of *Exile*. Gentle on her own time, ferocious in defense of her patients.

Ra'aila, Clan Flait. Aera. Captain of the TMS *Earthrise* at the time of *Exile*. She met Reese during the same incident that introduced Saul, on the planet of Kerayle during the novel *Rose Point*.

Saul Ferry. Hinichi. Mechanic and guard wolf. Saul meets Reese and Hirianthial on the colony world of Kerayle during the novel *Rose Point*; his actions there led Reese to offer him employment during the short story "The Call," which appeared in the collection *To the Court of Dragons*.

Sediryl Galare. Eldritch. The current heir to the

Eldritch empire, a mind-mage in her own right. Her origin story is told in the novel Girl on Fire, and her involvement in the Chatcaavan War begins in the novel Amulet Rampant.

Surapinet. Human. Former head of an interplanetary drug cartel; Reese Eddings got him imprisoned through her actions in the novel *Earthrise*.

Surela Silin Asaniefa. Eldritch. Antagonist to the aims of the Queen, Surela's attempt to take power saw her condemned as a traitor. She first appears in the novel *Rose Point*.

Thaniet Irys Asaniefa. Eldritch. Surela's dearly beloved lady-in-waiting, who was killed by Baniel's pirate allies. She appears (and meets her end) in the novel *Laisrathera*.

Theresa "Reese" Eddings. Human. The merchant and original captain of the TMS *Earthrise* who became a landed Eldritch noble during the events of the coup, as told in the Her Instruments series. Her story begins in the novel *Earthrise*.

"Third." Eldritch. Briefly mentioned during the conference at the beginning of Part 2, "Third" is the Chatcaavan title of Lisinthir Lauvet Imthereli, once Lisinthir Nase Galare, whose part in the war is explicated in detail in the Princes' Game series, beginning with *Even the Wingless*.

Thuliven Mel Deriline. Eldritch. Liolesa's Royal

Procurer, who was charged with helping her feed the populace. Became sympathetic to Surela during her short reign after assessing her motivations and personality; he appears briefly in the novel *Laisrathera*.

Twelveworld Lord. Chatcaavan. Lord over the historically significant and powerful Twelveworld area of the Chatcaavan Empire, he is currently detached to Eldritch space to aid their navy and search for traitorous Chatcaava who might have fled past the Eldritch world. He enters the story during the Princes' Game series, at the end of the novel *Amulet Rampant*.

"Val" Valthial Trena Firilith. Eldritch. The current male head of the Eldritch church, Val is a mind-mage who was involved in defeating the coup against Liolesa, with the aid of Reese Eddings and Hirianthial. He appears first in the novel *Laisrathera*.

THE ELDRITCH LANGUAGE

One of the unique features of the Eldritch language is the ability to modify the meaning of a word with emotional "colors." In the spoken language, these are indicated by the use of prefixes, which can be used as aggressively or as infrequently as the speaker desires; a single prefix can color an entire paragraph, or the speaker can use them to inflect every word. Uninflected language is considered emotionally neutral. These modifiers are not often used in the written language, but when they are, they take the form of colored inks.

There are three pairs of moods, with the gray mode not necessitating an opposite. Each mood in a pair is said to be the 'foil' of the other.

> **Gray (normal)** – No modifiers are required to denote the neutral mood, however there is a prefix associated with it, and using it can be interpreted as a way of calling attention to one's lack of mood.
> **Silver (hopeful)** – Silver Mode is the foil of the

Shadow mood, giving a positive flavor to words. This is the color of hope.

Shadowed (cynical) – When Shadowed, most words bear a negative connotation, usually cynical, sarcastic, or ironic. It can also be used for dread/foreboding or fear.

Gold (joyful) – The best is always assumed of everything in the Gold mood, and all words take on that flavor.

Black (dark) – Black, the foil of Gold, tends to violent, angry, or morose connotations of words. Whole groups of words radically change definition when referred to in the Black.

White (ephemeral/holy) – Whitened words refer to the spirit, to the holy and pure. You often find this mood used for weddings and in the priesthood, and in the schools that teach the handling of esper abilities.

Crimson (sensual) – The carnal mood gives words a sensual implication, and inflect speech to refer to things of passions and things of the body.

Eldritch is an aggressively agglutinating language: if it can make a word longer by grafting things onto it to add meaning, it will, and if that makes it harder for non-native speakers to pronounce anything without stumbling, so much the better. It's also fond of vowels, and almost inevitably if you see an Eldritch word with more than one adjacent vowel, they're pronounced separately. There are also no "silent" vowels (so Galare is not 'Gah lahr', but 'gah lah reh' or 'gah lah rey' depending on your regional accent). There are some cases where I've misspelled things, or I've continued to write out diphthongs instead of using diacritics, but for the most part if you pronounce every single letter you see in an Eldritch word separately, you'll probably be doing it right.

Like many of the languages of this setting, Eldritch was originally a conlang, created by the people who would become the Eldritch as a way to set themselves apart from the people they fled. It has been several thousand years since then, though, and the language has only become more convoluted since, a reflection of its people's needs.

AUTHOR SKETCHES

It's typical for me to do sketches while writing, a sort of mental doodling as I work out events and character arcs. These sketches are not intended to be the final word on what the characters look like! In fact, I usually have trouble pinning down people's looks. But I find I work better when I'm thinking with a pencil as well as a keyboard. Here are a few from my writing of *Shieldmatron 2*:

- *Kodo* - A quick doodle of the epigones. Their lower bodies are based on various large lizards, like komodo dragons.
- *Not Dying Here* - Some quick sketches from the middle section of the book; Fasianyl and her musician (name then uncertain), and Surela and Saul having A Moment.
- *Frustration* - Poor Surela, having yet another disagreement with Fasianyl. In the bottom left corner, Lunet is saying 'tsk'.

- *Lunet* - There's a lot of art of Lunet, but this is the most finished of them, a coloring sheet I did for Patreon of her with Bippity the Flitzbe.
- *Traitors* - Surela and Apex-Fleet.

GAENEN

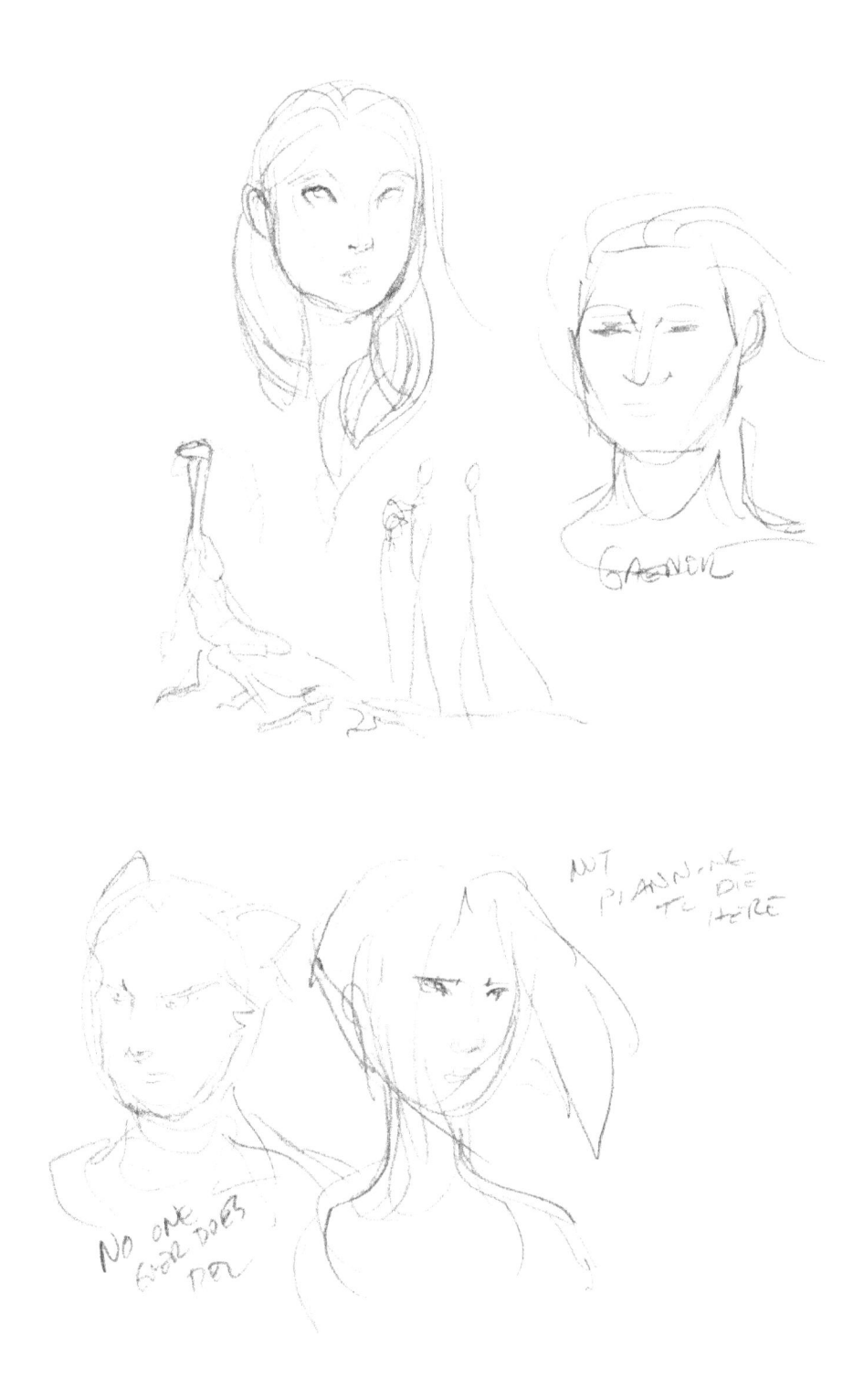

NOT PLANNING TO DIE HERE

NO ONE EVER DOES

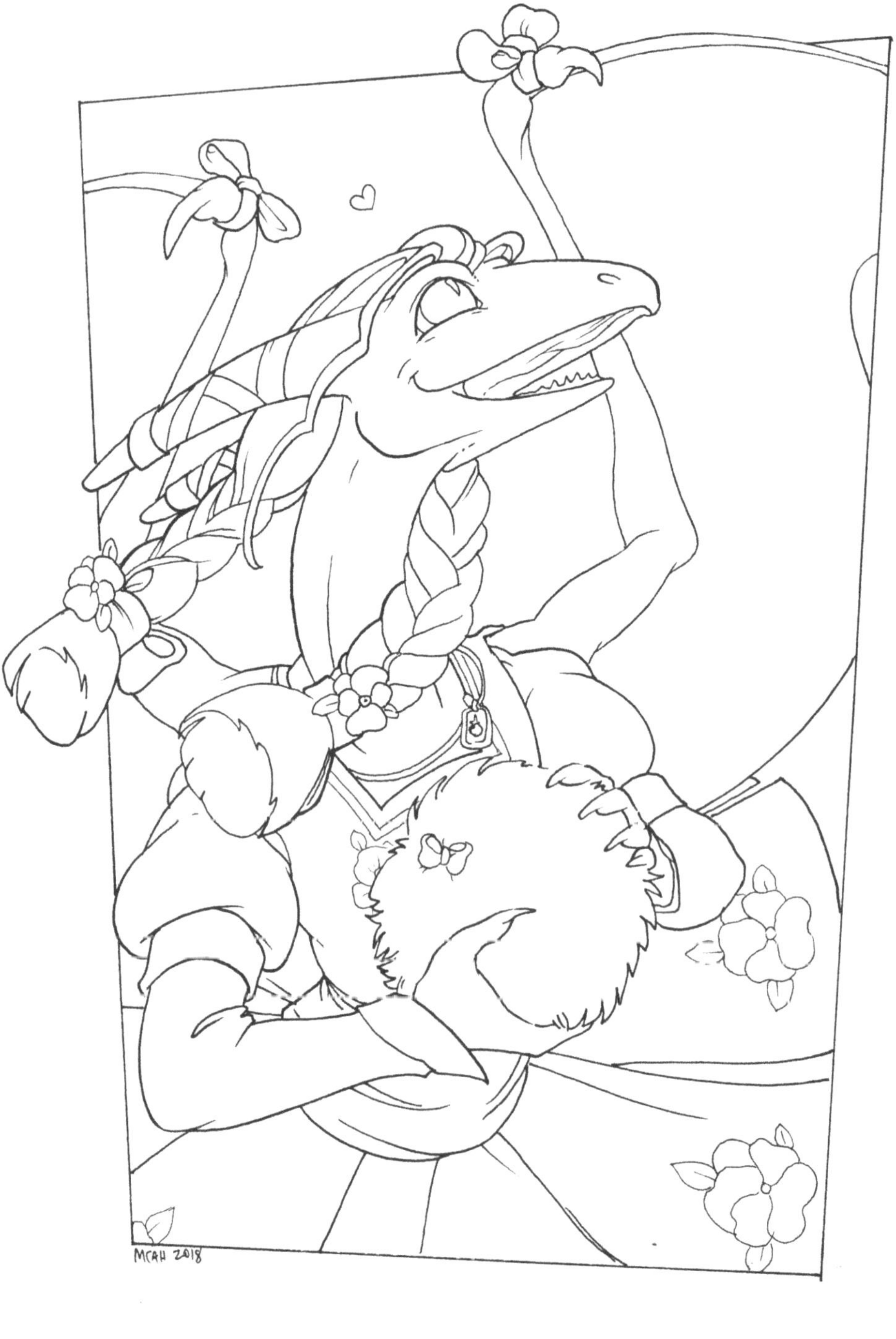
MCAH 2018

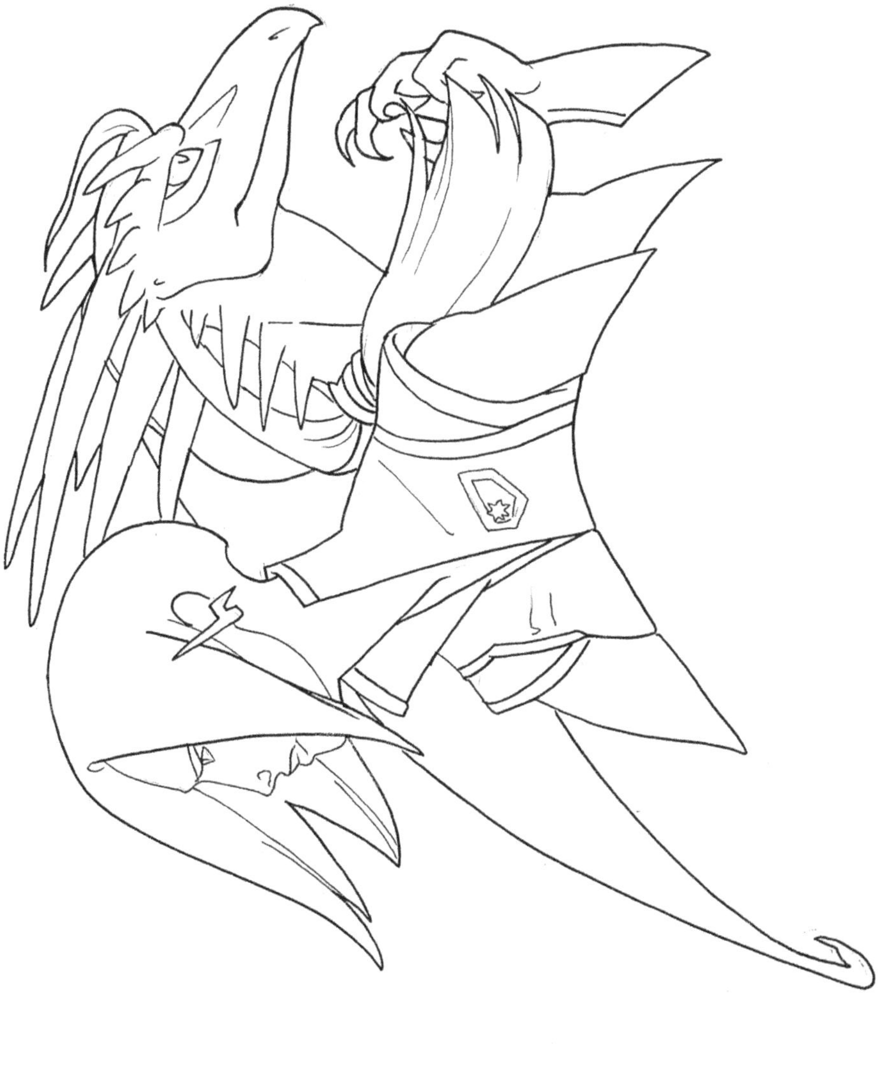

ACKNOWLEDGMENTS

Many thanks, as always to the following:

- My beta readers, who caught many typos and brought up useful issues: Bishopess, TS Davis, Josie, Julia and Martika, Brian, Karen, Sporky, Catherine, Kat, Engineer Sam, mrblanche, Sockeye, GrammyPuter, David, Amy, Jessica, Astrid, P Westling, and you, Anonymous. Any remaining errors and idiosyncrasies are certainly my own.
- Discord and Patreon/Locals patrons, for buying my groceries (and in some cases, additions to my ridiculous and unnecessary ink hoard—I'm looking at you, Petrov)
- Melissa McShane, who helpfully calculated how many words a day I'd have to write to make my deadline and didn't blink an eye at the resulting number. 'You can do it,' said she, and lo, I did...!

As always, much love to my family for their support, and for the Divine, all things.

ABOUT THE AUTHOR

Daughter of two Cuban political exiles, M.C.A. Hogarth was born a foreigner in the American melting pot and has had a fascination for the gaps in cultures and the bridges that span them ever since. She has been many things—web database architect, product manager, technical writer and massage therapist—but is currently a full-time parent, artist, writer and anthropologist to aliens, both human and otherwise. She is the author of over 60 titles in the genres of science fiction, fantasy, humor and romance.

An Exile Amid Stars is only one of the many stories set in the Pelted universe; more information is available on the author's website. You can also sign up for the author's quarterly newsletter to be notified of new releases.

If you enjoyed this book, please consider leaving a review... or telling a friend!

mcahogarth.org
mcahogarth@patreon
studiomcah@locals